WHAT IF WHAT'S INSIDE ME ISN'T ME?

by

MARK ENGELSSON

CONTENTS PAGE

FOREWORD &
ACKNOWLEDGEMENTS

This collection has been a long time coming, arguably since I first put pen to paper nearly twenty years ago. I've always been a words person; playing with language and imagery is second nature to me. The chance to use it as a way to vent the chaos of a troubled mind didn't hurt either.

Work began on this collection in February 2022, as a series of Google Drive folders. I selected what I felt were my best pieces and soon enough had a reasonable number, divided into a smattering of relatively light poems among the darker ones which reflect my more usual mind state. Then came the "fun" (I use this term with just a hint of sarcasm) task of editing and putting them into some semblance of order.

After much help along the way, what you have in your hands is the result of much deliberation and decision- making. I can proudly say that this collection is a good representation of my journey as a writer, encompassing various facets of my writing. The poems themselves may seem diverse, but they all come from one mind and make up parts of who I am and how I view the world. There are a number of themes that can be drawn from the poems, but I leave that task to your capable hands, dear reader.

I have, for those interested, attached notes at the end of this collection explaining some background on the poems – origins, influences and the like. These are obviously not required reading, but they may illuminate a little for those curious to dive deeper.

As anyone who has put together a book knows, it's not a one-person operation. While obviously the brunt of the writing falls on one pair of shoulders, there are many individuals who lend a hand (or two) along the way in order to turn an idea into a reality. Such is the case with this book, and it behooves me to thank them for their contribution in making *What If What's Inside Me Isn't Me?* what it is.

Firstly, the genesis of this book would not have come about without the endless support and feedback from Nicole Kunefke, Sam Patterson, and Lydia Wright, who were instrumental in their guidance and suggestions. I am also grateful for the work done by Tell Tell Poetry, who helped with the overall ordering of the poems and unveiling of the uniting themes, and indebted to Alyssa Harmon for her insightful edits, last-minute superhero antics and overall hype-woman status. This book would also look nowhere near as snazzy as it does without the help of Christine Caruana for the cover, with whom I am honored to have been able to work.

And finally, I dedicate this book to my partner, Nadia, who inspires me every day, and our three fluffs.

PETRICHOR

I love the smell of rain cascading from the heavens.

It's the scent of promise, of growth.

It speaks to me in whispers of the possibility that

all can be renewed.

It brings a time of cleansing;

Sins are forgotten, heartache is soothed.

The drizzle trickles down my face like the caress

of a loved one, caring and affectionate.

It ruffles my hair like an older relative.

Gray clouds watch over me like guardian angels.

Don't speak, just stand in the rain

And let it absolve you of your pains.

Allow your clothes to cling to you

Like a frightened child needing comfort.

Save your breath, and let the rain speak for you.

A MAP OF THE WORLD

A map of the world adorns his face;

Watch him aggravated as oceans boil.

The bumps and contours of a teenage boy,

Scarred, scraped, scratched, soiled.

Tears aflame streak down dusty canals,

Scorching remnants of a once-pink plain.

Now a cinder and glassed to marble;

Mangled, mashed, mired, maimed.

Continents contort with every expression,

As unpredictable as the weather's course.

Wrinkles crease into mountain ridges;

Confused, calamitous, capricious, coarse.

Tangled thorns to make the hair;

Untamed, lying scattered and piled.

Falling like streams to cover his eyes;

Worldly, woeful, wishful, wild

WAITING

Look around at all these people

Walking, sitting, waiting senselessly,

Or maybe purposelessly is a better description

But why wait to be given a purpose?

Have they not heard of the scarcity of time?

A precious commodity that everyone has

but few use effectively.

And whilst they sit patiently,

Engaging in inane chit-chat,

Or gazing into the distance,

The air reeks of procrastination

and missed opportunities,

Sailing past their front door like trash in the wind

DOWN WE GO

I punched myself in the face last night,

Just to see if the nerves still work.

Flashes of red in the back of my head,

Before the dulling monochrome sets in again.

It's not long before I'm back to old habits,

So satisfying a feeling to rip off plasters.

The scabs tearing free, quick count one-two-three,

They leave sore spots in a warm pinkish hue.

Fighting the urge to dig deeper,

But the itch is growing and it shows,

Spreading thin across my fragile skin,

And whispering of desires to go onward.

How far down does the rabbit hole go?

Down we go,

Separate the flesh from bone,

What's trapped inside me must be free,

But what if what's inside me isn't me?

JANTE LAW

Erase these images in my head;

Dreams shot down as they took flight.

Now they'll never see the light of day,

Buried deep under the ground,

Eyes peer out behind a smoking gun.

The haunting glares of disappointment

Stalk my every bid to succeed.

When every struggle is an uphill battle,

And a looming sense of disaster,

It leaves me wondering if this life is worth it.

Give me a chance to start over again,

Rewind my cassette to the start,

Ruined spools of tape,

The director's wrong choices,

Hindsight can teach so much,

But too late.

Maybe one day I'll find my purpose,

And my dreams can reach out beyond the
clouds.

DIAMONDS

There's more to life than happiness:
Looking into the Sun will blind you,
But its indirect pursuit: there's the trick.

Keep pushing through life's pain,
Withstand the mounting pressure,
And grow from the experience.

That's the thing with diamonds:
The more trauma you put them through,
The brighter they eventually shine.

Until they encrust a crown's jewels
Or a tower's highest spires,
Reflecting back the sunlight.

You and I can always be so much more,
And achieve so much more,
Than the graphite in this pencil.

SIGNAL TO NOISE RATIO

Metal fragments scatter

in a spiral on the floor;

magnetized, manipulated

by a strong surrounding force.

Twisting, the fragments scream

as they scratch the surface,

like moths to their flaming demise,

drawn closer to the source.

They cling to each other symbiotically,

for what source can exist

without its masses to gather?

And the shards grow thicker in turn.

The screams of the fragments

Only serve to mask the signal.

LET GO

Hold high the candle,
Shine into every dark corner
Of my bullet-riddled soul, brush away
All the dust, keep the cobwebs at bay.

Finding creatures that look like me,
Beasts that snarl with twisted expressions,
Screaming at you, before melting
Into a friendly façade as they bid you welcome.

Enter the masterpiece
Center-stage in the life-production:
A tank, what appears to be a tank
With someone inside, no water,
Pounding on the glass, but you can't
Hear his shouts, and it's odd because
This figure looks familiar in your eyes.
You realize, you *have* his eyes
It's the same person trapped inside.

You step up to the glass, stare deep inside,
Is it a reflection you're looking at of
Your soul or just your body?
Too late! The eyes have trapped you;
You're locked into his gaze.

Instantly you understand, he is no clone,
He *is* you, at least the part you choose to hide,
Occasionally released, with colossal damage.

So the side that you think is me,
Is actually incomplete, there's a fraction gone.
I'll let you decide, as I leave you here,
Your choice of my split personalities.
If you want to leave, try and bypass the beasts,
They're created every time he gets free.
It means that it's easier to beat him back.
Judging by the look on your face, you didn't know,
But eventually you can keep this part locked
Up for good. You just have to let loose every
Once in a while.

MIRROR

Wander down this hallway

Doors locked on both sides

Shadows, dust and echoes

Paint peels everywhere

There's a mirror hanging

Webs adorn its frame

Shuffling with reluctance

Stop and stare in fear

Watching your reflection

Haggard and forlorn

Skin is cracked and broken

Graying in the light

Mirror, mirror on the wall

Who is this?

The person that you knew

no longer exists

TECHNOCRACY

This all started long before you were born:

The struggle of titans, between capital and labor.

Cut-throats that cut throats to make a quick buck-fifty,

Sliced corners form a perfect circle, the cheapest you can find.

It's happened before and it'll happen again,

Society is shifting, spin on a dime,

All due to the Internet, a "powerful tool",

Quickly turned into a world wide web of deceit.

The vast human database, users its food:

Pushed from the top, spied on from the bottom.

Your toaster has your email, your kettle knows your friends,

And your oven serves you capitalism (this time it tastes like chicken).

Knowledge is power, who knows where we're headed?

Those at the top put their heads in the sand.

What did we do in defiling this technocracy?

So much potential, snatched away in the iron grip of a new regime.

This is your future,

Your new subscription starts now,

Whether you like it or not.

TIME

Uh oh, it's doing that thing again
Time is speeding up imperceptibly
Blink and you miss a day, a week
A month, a year, a lifetime
Your life is flashing before your eyes
Disappearing in a flurry of activity
OnYouMasSnapTwitFacePinstagram
Everyone rushing to be someone somewhere
Untilitgetstothepointyoucan'tevenbreathe
Andyou'rejustyellingSTOOOOOOOOP

Your voice echoes loud in the void
Everything is at a standstill
People stare at each other, wondering
Where did all of the busyness go?
What happened to all of this... stuff?
And so, life resumes at a slower pace
Folks take their time over decisions
Reconnect with that which makes us human
But it's only a matter of time before
It will start to speed up again

THREE SLOGANS

Why do your own research,
When you can get everything you need
From the man in the box?
He's so smart, he never steers us wrong
And flashing on the screen
Is that familiar phrase, all meaning lost
IGNORANCE IS STRENGTH

Technology evolves at a rate of knots
Data flies by at lightning speed
Zipping from spot to spot, a watchful eye
Machines buzz in our pockets
Keeping us safe by knowing us well
Emblazoned on cases in bedazzling gold
FREEDOM IS SLAVERY

The world will turn as it has always done
Humans will repeat history ad nauseam
As the troops once again march through city streets
Resplendent in their identical uniforms
Men, women and children cheer on their heroes
Smiling sadly as they chant the old maxim:
WAR IS PEACE

THE DOOR CLOSES

Don't give me that look

You and I both know this is over

And it was your decision

That made it abundantly clear

"Swear on my mother's grave"

Let her rest in peace

She doesn't need your whining

And frankly neither do I

The path is set, the door is closed

Our paths diverge at this point

You must go your own way

Without another word spoken

Leave, we need each other no longer

Take your time and heal from this

And remember one thing, above all:

There are plenty of other doors open for me

THE REUNION

After ten years, you'd think something
Would have etched on their faces,
And yet everyone from my school
Looks the same as they did.

Same photos, same vacant smiles,
Suited and booted or relaxing on beaches.
Dressed to the nines or holiday snaps;
Uniform profiles recall uniform days.

The bullies have learned little,
The teachers even less,
All the victims have to show
Are their therapy bills

It's not long before the gossiping starts;
Who's off the rails, and who's back on track.
A few popped the question, others popped out kids
(Whether intentionally or accidentally).

In ten years, nothing has changed,

Though I can't say I'm especially surprised;

I'll see you all in ten years,

For more of the same.

AND ALL THAT IT ENTAILS

In a bar on the main drag

A couple sit and wonder aloud

About the meaning of life

And all that it entails

The coffee machine whirs

To itself in the corner

Trying to discern its purpose

And all that it entails

A sigh and a cough

He knows his gruesome fate

As he takes a drag of smoke

And all that it entails

A young woman, steaming cup in hand

And a chair opposite, still empty

She wonders at the time of his arrival

And all that it entails

NO INTRODUCTION

Lack of interaction is my status quo

It's haunted me for as long as I know

I waited for people to say who they are

Or squinted at name-tags from afar;

That way they thought I cared about them

I walk along the prison yard,

Stares bore through my eyes, into my soul

Everyone knows why I'm here, what I've done

A twist of irony, no need for introduction

They all know my name, they will forever
know my name

He greets me with a warm smile, dead eyes

There's a sterile odor, a secret to hide

Though the room's purpose is abundantly clear

As he breathes the words I never wanted to hear,

"Prisoner number 435, come to the electric chair."

THE PASSENGER

As lights flash by overhead
I grip the steering wheel tightly
My wrists ache from the strain
Of not punching the passenger.
I guess that's what happens with
Carpool tunnel syndrome.

PASSION'S INFERNO

So much havoc wrought on such a small frame
Incinerated beyond recognition, a blend of
X's and Y's, identity: unknown. All that remains is
The pain, oh, the pain, still burning, continuing
Years after the flames were extinguished, when he left.

Scorched skin burnt by love's intensity
Eyes all pointing to one guilty source, a
Veritable, upstanding member of society, by all accounts
Except he is acting so coldly, his alibi flimsy.
Not as flimsy as the building they found the body in.

"Perhaps it was collateral, no harm intended
Everybody makes mistakes, but I confess the
Recipient of the burn was not the intended victim."
Collateral indeed, for who would have thought that
Even such a docile being could be caught up in passion's inferno,
Neglected, resulting in a blazing fire in their heart and now
The dead eyes of the wounded stare forlornly at the ceiling.

IN THE HEART OF THE WOODS

In the heart of the woods
A buried secret lies
Some object to be protected
A capsule of another time

'Twas placed there by a people
Ancient, fair and wise
Who made a simple error
That multiplied in size

Engraved on this capsule
In a language that did not survive
Are these eight simple words -

*"DO NOT TOUCH — WE ARE NO
LONGER ALIVE"*

A metal detector beeps
"Some treasure in the ground!"
The little boy stands over the hole
And lifts what he's found

He peers at this cylinder
Fiddles with the lights
A blinding flash bursts out
And robs him of his sight

He drops it with all haste
And runs back to the house
The capsule slowly opens
A mist comes pouring out

A BREAKDOWN OR A BREAKTHROUGH?

I wake to another Sisyphean nightmare;

Rolling this rock is so

So, tiresome. The path is well-worn

By now, trodden to mud.

Up and down, up and down, enough

to make even the Grand Old Duke blush.

My muscles bulge

and strain under the boulder's weight.

Until finally, one day, something clicks

or does it snap?

Is this a breakdown or a breakthrough?

And can it really be that simple

to just... walk away?

ON THE SIDE OF THE ROAD

I saw a dead tabby cat

on the side of the road,

body stretched out in mid-flight.

Its intestines were spilled out next to it

like baked beans

a fixed expression of panic

from when the thoughtless driver hit it

I wonder what its final thoughts were

As the wheels crunched

Through its bones;

A fear of the oncoming, or a plea for help.

A lone ranger, or a part of a wider clowder.

Out on the hunt or headed to home turf.

Now left on display

on the side of the road

Its spirit crushed from its frame.

WATCHING AS THEY EXHALE DEATH

Pools of light from rows of vehicles

Spill out across the concrete jungle

Merciless eyes, glaring at strangers,

And pipes at the back, watching as they exhale death

Tendrils curl as they huff out their waste

Fumes are rising from bottomless pits

Filled with rotten teeth and slimy tongues

With knowing intent, watching as they exhale
death

Looming towers oversee their kingdom

Hostages held in captivity by mankind's greed

As power new is sought to replace waning old

The plumes still rise, watching as they exhale
death

Smoke streams out behind as the machines fly on

The nightly run to eliminate the unknown foe

Propellers whirr as bullets whiz past

Humans are falling, watching as they exhale death

ALICE IN NIGHTMARELAND

The wine is on the table,

The poison in the chalice,

The apple has a bite mark;

This is all too much for Alice.

The castle walls are looming,

Within the confines of her palace,

She shreds her voice with screaming;

This is all too much for Alice.

The paintings are conspiring,

Driving her insane with malice.

Their glaring eyes and spreading lies;

This is all too much for Alice.

She beats against the table,

Drains that golden chalice,

Throws the apple to her dogs;

This is all too much for Alice

The wooden doors burst open,

Their force shatters the ballast.

She makes a break, she will escape;

This is all too much for Alice

Water drips from cracks above.

Her feet are wrecked from cut and callus

Sitting, rocking, in a padded cell,

This was all too much for Alice.

THE BOG-DWELLER

The carrion stench is pervasive
It poisons the water with blood
Tendrils swirl from the bodies
Spreading, rippling outwards
To sink down into the depths
While these corpses remain
Rigid, suspended in place
In time, they will become
Food for the bog-dweller
Hiding in the tamaracks
Watching and waiting
For the next time it
Attacks there'll be
Not a single trace
Left, a clear way
Enough to entice
Another mortal
Curious, naïve
Walks this way
To meet their
Fatal quietus,
Descend to
Eternally
Lie as a
Carcass
Devoid
Of all
Life

WATERY GRAVE

Along a beach at night I wander,
The sea enshrouded by the light of the moon.
In mind and body I feel naked,
I stand before my judgment.

Wretched sea, come claim my life,
I'll embrace these waves of anguish.
And how was I to know
They'd pull me under?

And so I step into the ocean,
Feeling its cold and welcome arms
Envelop me in a world of numbness,
My body licked with icy tongues.

Onward and onward I will walk,
Until my body's encased in ice,
And then the sea will drag me down
Its lips to rob me of my final breath

LET PAIN BE YOUR GUIDE

A portrayal of guilt

Porcelain fractures

Across her innocent face

The terror of discovery

And of damage done

These deeds will echo

For hundreds of years

And the words will rot

Six feet deep

Within her skin

Deep breath. Breathe again.

Swallow the water down

This self-sacrifice is in vain

To live is to suffer

Let pain be your guide

THE SAME GRAVE

Look around
Everything has fallen to pieces
It's ruined, all ruined
The beast has come, ravaged the ground
While we clamored for more

The world's a smoldering husk
of its former self
Never to reclaim its beauty
A pile of ashes and rubble
Frozen in the extinguished sun

How long ago was it?
Time passes by so strangely
No hope of resurrection
Nor spark to reignite
The debris remains for all eternity

We will rot in the same grave
We will rot in the same grave
We will rot in the same grave

SACRIFICE

Saddened faces, empty faces
Angry, screaming, wordless faces
Powerless, placid, docile faces
Eyes boring a hole into my soul

"Forget us," into the abyss they are thrown
"Leave us," but they will never be alone
"Forgive us," but redemption is unknown
"Destroy us," when destruction is their home

Begging people, desperate people
Tortured, oppressed, damaged people
Persecuted, helpless people
Tears streaming as acid on my soul

"Forget us," into the abyss they are thrown
"Leave us," but they will never be alone
"Forgive us," but redemption is unknown
"Destroy us," when destruction is their home

"The tears of a thousand people washed the
soil clean; clean of the stains and the dirt and
the horror of what was witnessed. They lay
down to forge a new beginning for another
people. They were forgotten, but their sacrifice
was not."

THE DRIVE

The drive to live,

The spark to strive,

The flame to achieve,

Burning down the wick.

But what happens when the fire

Expires,

Suffocates,

Is snuffed out?

And the eyes that contained it

Fade to a glassy version

Of their former selves?

WHERE WERE YOU WHEN YOU GAVE UP?

Where were you when you gave up?
When your dreams crawled out of your headspace
and died, shivering, starved of nourishment?

Where were you when you abandoned ship?
When your hopes of building a legacy crumbled
and were left to gather dust in the corner?

Where were you when you stopped caring?
When your ideals became compromised
and you lost sight of that which drove you onward?

Where were you when everything shut down?
When your sense of self evaporated into air
and all you had left was a shell of what was?

BREATHE IN AND OUT

The operation of hauling in air
Is an act taken for granted;
Life floods into lungs, expanded,
So vital yet done without a care.

With breath we weave tales to inspire
Paint our mental tapestries
Patterns form as we respire
That adorn or stain memories

Have you ever considered as you're breathing
What exactly rushes inside?
Some of it harming, some of it healing
And some we won't know 'til we've died

The coolness of air in the evening
Or humidity of the day
The former can be relieving
The latter obstructs your way

So, think on your next inhalation
Just what kind of air did you breathe?
And during the last exhalation
Watch the life that you're living now leave

THE INVENTED GOD

« *"If God did not exist, it would be necessary to invent him."* »

- Voltaire

And so we did:

Magicked him out of thin air,

Fabricated from the cloths of a thousand stories,

Made him in our own image,

With the same fatal flaws that plague our existence.

Insipid writer I am not,

Merely jaded by the calcified views of the blinded masses.

I look up at the three portraits of the imposters,

And see only smudged sketches

Of *Ecce Mono* and its poor attempts at inspiring servitude.

If your lodging is filled with lizards and rats,

You only have yourself to blame.

No gods, no masters are your landlords.

So clean up your own house,

And rely not on preterist views as your guide.

But when all is said and done,

Take this as nothing more than persiflage,

And as the years pass on,

One fairytale will be exchanged for another.

The battle of wills rages on forever.

DESERT REBIRTH

Moving into focus

Hazy shadows of red

No signs of life around

As they carry their dead

They trudge across the plains

Each step weaker than the last

Their brows furrowed with pain

Sunlight scorches the sandblast

One falters, collapses, falls to the ground

Flies on the body swirl in a horde

The casket shatters, spills all around

Spin tighter and tighter, they start to transform

A new body steps forth, reborn from the swarm

The carriers decompose, piles on the sand

While the body shuffles on of its own accord

Leaving scraps of cloth across the land

DEATH AS A WOMAN ON THE UNDERGROUND

I saw death as a woman on the Underground

With a smile on her lips sweet as sin

And dressed up, glitz and glamor abound

Her angelic face belies the devil within

She fixed me a look in the eye as if to say

That life is short, enjoy the ride

When you come to the end of the day

Make sure you're happy with the course of your life

In that moment I knew this was all a joke

Our existence flawed and full of holes

When I next looked, she was gone in the smoke

Replaced by those yellowing pock-riddled poles

An old woman sat there, looking so wilted

She realized her time was long spent

Her bejeweled tiaras and life so gilded

Were signs of where the wasted hours went

I smiled knowingly at this poor lady's fortune

And admired my hopefully long years to come

For though life's music may seem in such poor tune

It all comes to harmony when your song is done

O WORLD! I REMAIN NO LONGER HERE

O world! I remain no longer here:

My body and spirit hath divorced.

But weep not for this loss of ours;

I leave this place with no remorse.

O world! I remain no longer here:

No chains will hold me down.

But hold a celebration, not a wake

When I am buried in the ground.

O world! I remain no longer here:

There is another place that I must be.

But think not that this is premature;

My mind, it soars, spirit free.

O world! I remain no longer here:

I am laid to rest, with eyes closed tight.

But live your life, seize every day,

Until once more we reunite.

THE LONELY TREE

Out on a barren hilltop,

Overlooking dip and vale,

There stands a lonely tree;

Its bony hands are weak and frail.

Its body has been battered

By many a tempest and howling gale.

No leaves remain in sight;

Its roots begin to fail.

And where this lonely tree has fallen

Its child will grow in its place,

To carry on the former's legacy:

A task that it will willingly embrace.

HOME

Follow the journey of a man so proud:

Guide me on my way

Stepping out the door

Cross each field and mountain high

Through each vale and fjord

Sing the song of a choir so proud:

Nature's summer ensemble

Dimmed by autumn winds

And the icy winter spires

Melt to brooks of spring

Embrace the spirit of a land so proud:

From the snow on peaks

To foam built up on shore

Let me flow where it takes me

Life without encore

Though far and wide on this Earth we may roam

We carry a piece of this place we call home

SHE

In surrounding darkness, a bright flame burns

This fiery creature, arms outstretched

A look of determination, to conquer the storm

White-hot passion, to live this life to the fullest

Nothing will stop her or stand in her way

As she slices her way through life's tribulations

Every jungle falls to her glistening scythe

Leaving a path to where no one has gone before

She keeps demons at bay that would swallow her whole

Without showing an inkling of fear

A fighter, resolute to the bitter end

Bold, strong, ready to take on any obstacle

You make survival feel so beautiful

You make me want to live again

ON A WINTER'S MORNING, DEATH TOOK HER BY THE HAND

On a winter's morning

Death took her by the hand

And led her over snowy fields

The iciness of his embrace

Reminded her of a lover

She knew she was in safe hands

They traversed over dale and stream

And wandered over many hills

A last reminder of this world's beauty

So when they found her body

Frozen still under the lake

A smile played on her face

TEN THOUSAND STRONG

(In Honor of Maya Angelou)

I come as one,
I stand as ten thousand.

A product of all
my circumstances.
The sum of all
my experience.
A tapestry of all
I have witnessed,
and all I have done.

Power within, unbridled,
tingles in my fingers
and warms my soul.
It radiates from my core,
illuminates the faces
of those I have met.

No step that I take
is ever alone.

I walk with strength,
with purpose, with love.
What once was war inside,
now is only peace
and harmony.

Through my eyes,
I see the world in
kaleidoscopic vision;
every moment captured,
every feeling preserved,
in the mosaic of my being.

Humble, yet firm
I plant my feet
and will not be moved.
No matter the tempest,
my inner self is calm,
safe in the knowledge
that I am worthy,
that I am I.

I come as one,
I stand as ten thousand.

CAMPFIRE CIRCLES

Step out of the circle now
It's your time to shine, my child
The stars have aligned in your favor
The path is laid out before you

Go with the grace of the gods
Walk away with your head held high
Do not let your footsteps falter
When your journey has already begun

Oh, you've only just realized?
Well, best be on your way then
At least, there is one thing we can provide
Time — soon enough its value will be clear

Waste no time on the what ifs
You'll try them again on the next go around
Know that life moves in mysterious ways
Stay ready for whatever may come

We will sit here in the campfire circle
Patiently awaiting your return
As we have always done

NOTES

You might be wondering why I have some blank pages at the end of the book. For those who like to take notes on what they have read in the book, this can be a section for your own personal thoughts, to let your own creativity flow... or just to write a phone number. If you buy this book for a loved one, maybe here you can leave a message for them here with your thoughts on specific poems. Have fun!

"Art is in the eye of the beholder, and everyone will have their own interpretation."

— E.A. Bucchianeri, Brushstrokes of a Gadfly

» Petrichor

I wanted to start off the collection with one of the few "happier" poems, which holds a fairly simple and straightforward concept I'm sure many can relate to. Nature comes up a fair bit in my poetry, both in lighter and darker tones.

» A Map Of The World

The origin of this one is quite amusing – a friend of mine posted a photo of himself with wild hair and beard having taken part in some color festival. The image struck me deeply and conjured this image of the world as man. Thanks to Dylan Schink for the image. I had great fun playing with the structure here, especially the alliteration of each stanza's last line and the vivid imagery inspired by this photo.

» Waiting

I actually have very little memory of writing this poem or its circumstances, but I can hazard a guess that it was in relation to a less-than-delightful town where I spent a chunk of my life. It's not exactly the most inspiring place. I dug it up and gave it a lick of paint, and it was ready to roll.
Most of my earlier poems are in four-or-five-line stanzas, as I lacked the confidence to branch out from such rigid lines. This was one of my earlier attempts to break that mold.

» Down We Go

Believe it or not, this first stanza was sort of modeled off Nine Inch Nails' "Hurt", before then spinning off into different if no less evocative territory. There was a whole section of repetition in an earlier version of this poem, but it got axed as I didn't feel it was strong enough.

» Jante Law

I remember the origins of this poem around my late teens, when I first heard about Jante Law (also known as Tall Poppy Syndrome and several other terms). I found it interesting that this term – which I initially assumed to be idiosyncratically Nordic – is actually international. I find it remarkable that we as a species often have this predisposition to speak negatively of others' successes, finding any excuse to explain it away as luck or privilege (though in some cases that may be true!). We could achieve so much more if this negativity weren't the case, and we lifted each other up.

Like much of my writing from this period, I took a fair bit of inspiration from the music I was listening to (this will be a common theme across many of my notes). I can see hints of Tim McIlrath (Rise Against et al.) in here as part of my punk rock days.

» Diamonds

I've always found the notion of carbon fascinating – how a basic material can make up such vastly different end products, used in different ways and valued at such different price points. I'm quite proud of the symbolism in this poem.

» **Signal To Noise Ratio**

Another poem which was quite heavily inspired by a couple of different artists – in one, the soundscape and in another the lyrical style. The soundscape comes from industrial band Locrian – their album *Infinite Dissolution* informed the clinical and mechanical style that informs the earlier part of the poem. The rest of the lyrical influence comes from another mainstay of my listening habits, melodic death metal pioneers Dark Tranquility. I love the immediate and intense stylings of Mikael Stanne's writing.

» **Let Go**

This is one of the poems I was most proud of around the time that I finished writing it, and I remember showing it to a number of friends – one of the first cases of me taking that step beyond the confines of my own writing space, though I was definitely not writing for an audience. The concept initially grew from a fascination with the movie *The Prestige*. While there are some things that I'd maybe have phrased differently now, I've chosen to leave it virtually untouched from its original form because I feel it captures a certain time and place in my mental state.

» **Mirror**

A relatively new piece that could also work as a lyric should I wish to put vocal melodies to it (a lot of my poetry is also written with a lyrics approach in mind). The final stanza was reworked from an Ulver track – such a wonderful band – and the rest grew out of it organically. I spent a long time on syllable patterning with this one, and I think it pays off in a fairly catchy yet dark piece.

» **Technocracy**

Ah, the misguided politics of youth. A few neat turns of phrase (I've always liked *"cut-throats that cut throats to make a quick buck-fifty"*), but you can tell this is one of my earlier pieces due to the general lack of political clarity. Still, I included it as an example of the sardonic wit I was shooting for.

» **Time**
Inspired by one of my favorite modern poets, Brian Bilston. His witty approach to subject matter is impressive, and I thought to put my own spin on a similar concept. The concept of time is something I struggle with at the best of times – life really does feel like a rollercoaster.

» Three Slogans

I was so happy I finally managed to create a poem related to those famous maxims from *1984*. It's a book I firmly believe should be read by everyone – when they are at the right age to read it, of course, and that in itself is up for debate. It had a profound effect on me both when I first read it, and the subsequent times I've gone back to it. The poem is perhaps not the most original piece, but it's one of my most honest ones.

» The Door Closes

Like many of the poems in this collection, they will germinate from a small seed of an idea, usually a line or two that then expands until it feels as done as it can be. In this case I was playing with the idea of swearing on something so serious, and wondering what the repercussions of this could be for the recipient parties.
The rest of the theme, sadly, comes from personal experience, and I'm sure is a topic many can identify with.

» The Reunion

Like many people, high school was not the happiest time for me, and the notion of going back to compare how everyone's lives have changed fills me more with dread than joy. Those with whom I have stayed in contact are more than enough of a positive reminder of my time there. Social media can be held to blame for the morbid curiosity that arises, that provides the answer to the question of, "Whatever happened to So-And-So?"

» And All That It Entails

This poem started from a painting that was hanging in my high school English classroom – "*Nighthawks*" by Edward Hopper (thanks Stephanie Jane for reminding me!) – involving a couple sitting at a bar. I built the rest of the scenario around the mise-en-scène and this titular phrase kept coming back to me. I don't use repetition often, but here it seemed appropriate.

» No Introduction

This one came about from one of those theme challenges I saw circling the Internet. It provided words or concepts and the idea was to see what sparked in the imagination from them. Knowing me, it wasn't long before it went down a darker path. I think I had watched *The Green Mile* at that point, which explains the 'electric chair' reference at the end.

» The Passenger

Nothing like a good pun that formed the basis of this short little number. If you wince, my job is done.

» Passion's Inferno

Same as above with regards to the theme challenges, this is one of my proudest achievements. I aimed for as smooth an acrostic as possible, and feel fairly confident that I nailed it. Still unsure whether the topic itself comes through as intended, but I'd prefer to leave it up to the reader how they wish to interpret it.

» In The Heart Of The Woods

One of my newer pieces, which started merely a play on imagery, and then was built upon for a more narrative-like approach as the story progresses. The patterning could do with a bit of work, but overall I quite like its vibe.

» A Breakdown or a Breakthrough?

There is poetry to be found everywhere you look – even in chance comments from friends. This one comes from a fellow poet, Jo Butler, who was describing the genesis of one of her poems at a local reading. I loved this quote and was immediately reminded of the Greek tragedy from which the poem sprang.

» On The Side Of The Road

Based on a true story! I went for a more stream-of-consciousness approach with this one, bored of the four-line stanza pieces that kept appearing. And any excuse to use the word 'clowder', really.

» Watching As They Exhale Death

A repetition piece which actually worked! This one had a bit of a brush-up as it was too abstract in the final stanza, but other than that has been left pretty much untouched from its teenage origins.

» Alice In Nightmareland

This one went through several iterations, as I recall. Took me ages to get the right phrasing and rhyme (so few convincing rhymes for Alice, a couple I squint at!) but that last stanza makes it worth it in my view. Definitely one of my darker pieces, and a highlight of my younger years.

» The Bog-Dweller

I haven't experimented much with shape poetry – not my style, really – but I couldn't resist the challenge of increasingly smaller lines. The first two lines of this poem were actually intended for a black metal lyric that never came to pass.

» Watery Grave

Like a lot of pieces around this period, I was fairly heavily influenced by the lyrical stylings of bands like Insomnium, who took their own influence from Poe et al. There are poems I didn't include which lean even more heavily on these influences, but this one is still a nice reminder for me of those times where I was still finding my feet and channeling the maelstrom of my mind.

» Let Pain Be Your Guide

Shamelessly hijacked the title of this from the band in the first line – Portrayal of Guilt, a fantastic heavy band. I listened to *Let Pain Be Your Guide* on repeat and did my best to portray (sorry) the emotions conveyed. I wrestled with the gender of the character for a while (and even considered 'they' to get around the issue, but it didn't scan right), so 'she' is how it shall be.

» The Same Grave

Started with the last line and pretty much worked backwards. Funny how things go. I took a lot of inspiration from chaotic hardcore vibes with a twist of metal anger. I didn't necessarily write it as lyrics in mind, but it could probably work as a lyric to the right music.

» Sacrifice

Another one where I have absolutely no recollection of writing this – especially the last bit. I was even so convinced I had taken it from somewhere that I tried Googling for it, but alas… it seems to be my own work. Applying a retrospective view on it, it may have been informed about some World War history I was studying at the time.

» The Drive

I think this came from another of ideas from the theme challenge that sparked No Introduction et al. A fairly simple piece that drives (sorry) home the hopeless narrative I was so embroiled in. In some ways this piece could be connected with Passion's Inferno.

» Where Were You When You Gave Up?

This one came from a web comic (Calvin and Hobbes-esque, something in that vein at least) that I saw whose punchline became the title and first line here. Rule of three played a big part in writing this.

» Breathe In And Out

You ever thought about when you're manually breathing? Like that line from The Matrix that Morpheus says? Well, I took that thought for a wander, maybe just a little too far on this one. Nothing like a bit of morbid musing.

» The Invented God

I was extremely hesitant to put this poem in, as I know that it is likely to make many uncomfortable. However, I am also fairly proud of it as my personal answer to Voltaire's writings. It may not make much sense if you don't read the original text (entitled *Epistle to the author of the book, "The Three Impostors",* easy enough to find online based on the quote included), so I encourage that if you are curious to dive deeper.

» **Desert Rebirth**

Thanks to the band DOEM for the soundtrack for this piece. Purely drawn from the imagery that their song "The Fly" conjured. I also took some inspiration from Sleep's *Dopesmoker* album cover.

» **Death As A Woman On The Underground**

I have wracked my brains for the origins of this poem, and I honestly cannot recall where it came from. It definitely appeared around my high school age, that's all I can remember. Anyway, fairly chuffed with it, especially the rhyme scheme.

» **O World! I Remain No Longer Here**

Title half-inched from post-metal band Glacier – I liked the sentiment as well as the song, and so used it as a basis for this vaguely comforting meditation on death and what lies beyond.

» **The Lonely Tree**

Again, based off an image prompt, and with a hopeful twist at the end. See, some happiness in my writing!

» Home

This piece was spawned by a painting from a good friend of mine, Virpi Thornton, which I believe one of us referred to as "Norway". Hence, I wrote a poem about Norway. It's not my home (not that anywhere is really my home, but that's another story), but there is something so powerful and inspiring about this place. I try to imagine what it's like to call a place home, especially a place with such beauteous nature as Norway.

» She

Dedicated to my partner. The last two lines came to me at some point, and I toyed with the idea of turning it into a song. This emerged instead, and I am happy it did.

» On A Winter's Morning, Death Took Her By The Hand

Title stolen from a dungeon synth project entitled Vetus Sepulcrum. I wrote this during a particularly bleak day outside, having just finished reading a key scene in *Evgeny Onegin*, and the images I wrote about played in my head as I saw that song name.

» Ten Thousand Strong

I always found this quote by Maya Angelou to be motivational and thought-provoking. Asking a number of my friends how they interpreted this quote revealed a multitude of answers, all of which informed the directions taken in this piece (as well as my own thoughts). What's your take on it?

» Campfire Circles

And so, we come to the end of the collection. A final send-off after all these meditations on death, loss, identity and who knows what else. I find this piece kind of comforting: ancient wise ones sitting in a circle instructing the younglings before they are sent off into the wilderness, cyclical by its very nature. It's a fitting ending.

CONCLUSION

Thank you for your time in reading this collection of poems that mean so much to me. If you fancy leaving a review on Amazon or Goodreads, I would be exceptionally grateful.

If you want to get in touch, I would love to hear your feedback. Any comments allow me to constantly evolve and improve in my writing journey. So, drop me an email or hit me up on social media, and let's talk poetry.

Until next time.

Email: markengelssonwrites@gmail.com

Substack: markengelssonwrites.substack.com

Facebook: Mark Engelsson Writes

Instagram: @MarkEngelssonWrites

Twitter: @MarkEngelsson

TikTok: @MarkEngelssonWrites

Personal Notes

Printed in Great Britain
by Amazon